KT-503-755

This book belongs to

....

First published 2015 by Brown Watson
The Old Mill, 76 Fleckney Road
Kibworth Beauchamp
Leicestershire LE8 0HG
ISBN: 978-0-7097-2253-3
© 2015 Brown Watson, England
Reprinted 2015, 2016
Printed in Malaysia

The Night Before
Christmas

A Visit from St Nicholas

By Clement C. Moore

Illustrated by Gill Guile

Brown Watson

ENGLAND LE8 0HG

'Twas the night before Christmas, when all through the house
Not a creature was stirring, not even a mouse.

The stockings were hung by the chimney with care,
In hopes that St Nicholas soon would be there.

The children were nestled
all snug in their beds,
While visions of sugar-plums
danced in their heads.

And mamma in her 'kerchief, and I in my cap,
Had just settled our brains for a long winter's nap.

'When out on the lawn there arose such a clatter,
I sprang from the bed to see what was the matter.

Away to the window
I flew like a flash,
Tore open the shutters
and threw up the sash.

The moon on the breast
of the new-fallen snow
Gave the lustre of midday
to objects below.

When, what to my wondering eyes should appear,
But a miniature sleigh, and eight tiny reindeer.
With a little old driver, so lively and quick,
I knew in a moment it must be St Nick.

More rapid than eagles,
His coursers they came,
And he whistled, and shouted,
and called them by name:
"Now, Dasher! Now, Dancer!
Now, Prancer and Vixen!
On, Comet! On, Cupid!
On Donner
And Blitzen!

To the top of the porch, to the top of the wall!
Now dash away! Dash away! Dash away all!"

As dry leaves that before the wild hurricane fly,
When they meet with an obstacle, mount to the sky.
So up to the house-top the coursers they flew,
With the sleigh full of toys,
and St Nicholas too.

And then, in a twinkling, I heard on the roof
The prancing and pawing of each little hoof.
As I drew in my head, and was turning around,
Down the chimney St Nicholas came with a bound.

He was dressed all in fur,
from his head to his foot,
And his clothes were all tarnished
with ashes and soot.
A bundle of toys
he had flung on his back.
And he looked like a pedlar
just opening his pack.

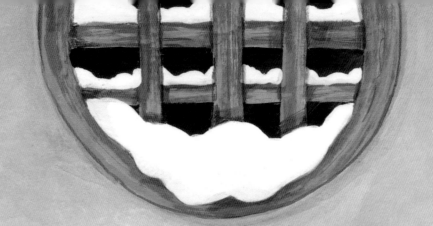

His eyes-how they twinkled! His dimples how merry!
His checks were like roses, his nose like a cherry!
His droll little mouth was drawn up like a bow,
And the beard of his chin was as white as the snow.

He had a broad face and a little round belly,
That shook when he laughed, like a bowlful of jelly!
He was chubby and plump, a right jolly old elf,
And I laughed when I saw him, in spite of myself!

A wink of his eye and a twist of his head,
Soon gave me to know I had nothing to dread
He spoke not a word, but went straight to his work,
And filled all the stockings, then turned with a jerk.

And laying his finger aside of his nose,
And giving a nod, up the chimney he rose!

He sprang to his sleigh,

to his team gave a whistle,

And away they all flew

like the down of a thistle.

But I heard him exclaim,
'ere he drove out of sight,
"Happy Christmas to all,
and to all a good-night!"